My Brother Daniel

My Brother Daniel

AND OTHER STORIES OF
BROTHERS AND SISTERS

Compiled by the Editors
of
Highlights for Children

Published by Highlights for Children, Inc.
P.O. Box 18201
Columbus, Ohio 43218-0201
Printed in the United States of America

ISBN 0-87534-625-1

CONTENTS

My Brother Daniel

By Joan Ebbeson

My brother Daniel told me once, "Whenever you wonder about something, just ask me. I *always* have an answer."

And he does, too.

On the side of the street near our house is a hole. A very deep, square hole with iron bars over it. One day I asked my brother Daniel what it was.

"That's a special kind of underground cage," he told me. "Dragons and dinosaurs are kept down in there."

When I told him that I thought all the dinosaurs had died a long time ago and there were no such things as dragons, he said, "A lot of people think so, because the dragons and dinosaurs never come out of their underground cages. You can't see them down there because it is so dark. And, of course, everyone *knows* they don't make a sound."

One day I saw a man with a truck next to the hole. A long hose was attached to the truck, and the end of it was down inside the hole. The iron bars had been taken off. I asked the man if he wasn't afraid of the dragons and dinosaurs.

"There are no dragons or dinosaurs, kid," he said. "I'm cleaning leaves out of this storm sewer."

When I told Daniel what the man said, he shook his head.

"The man just didn't want you to be scared. Of course, what he was doing was *feeding* the dragons and dinosaurs!"

And I really believed that.

My brother Daniel told me that way back in the corner of his bottom drawer, the one where he keeps his football cards, is an invisible lion. And when anyone besides Daniel opens that drawer, the lion jumps out and roars.

One day when Mom was putting away socks in my older brothers' room, she opened Daniel's bottom drawer by mistake. I hid behind the door and waited, but I didn't hear any roar.

When I asked Daniel about it he said, "Of course, I have trained the lion *not* to roar at Mother!"

I believed that.

My brother Daniel told me once that our dog, Fred, sings to him in the middle of the night, every night. I asked Daniel what songs Fred sings.

"Opera songs," said Daniel. "And he sings them in *Italian.*"

That night I stayed awake all night and listened for Fred's singing. But he didn't sing a single note.

"Of course," said Daniel the next morning. "Last night Fred had a sore throat."

I guess I believed that, too.

My brother Daniel told me that a little man lives inside the radio in the kitchen and that the man's job is to tell us the news and weather each morning. One day I peeked into the back of the radio to see the little man. But he wasn't there.

"Well, maybe the little man wasn't there at the *time,*" said Daniel. "He was probably out to lunch."

I didn't know whether to believe that or not.

Today, when we had show-and-tell at school, I brought a little blue eggshell that my brother had given me.

"My brother Daniel gave this to me," I told the class. "He got it from a little blue chick who didn't need it anymore. It was laid by a little magic hen. After the egg hatched, they both walked across the street to catch a bus."

"Your brother must have a great imagination," said Mrs. Wicks, my teacher.

"What's an imagination?" I asked Daniel when I saw him on the school bus.

"Why do you want to know?"

"Because Mrs. Wicks, my teacher, said you have a great imagination."

When we got home, Daniel showed me what an imagination is. I'd always thought that thing was called a hockey stick, but Daniel said it's an imagination. An imagination is a sort of magic wand shaped like a hockey stick. And when it's waved three times, it can make little brothers disappear.

I don't believe *that* at all!

The Mad Scientist

By Marlys G. Stapelbroek

It happened again last week when I turned in my project for the fourth-grade science fair.

"Andrea, what a marvelous idea!" my teacher said with a smile. "Why, I remember Eric's project three years ago."

I sighed. Eric is my big brother, and he's really good at science. The kids even call him the Mad Scientist. I get pretty tired of being known as Eric's kid sister, but after last weekend maybe I won't mind as much.

I was in the kitchen when Eric called to me from the hammock in the backyard.

"Hey, Squirt! Get me another soda."

"Get it yourself!" I shouted out the window. I hate it when he calls me Squirt.

"But I'm all comfortable."

"You're supposed to be mowing the lawn."

He groaned. "Could you at least get it out of the refrigerator for me?"

"OK," I grumbled, figuring I'd get one for myself, too.

"And bring it over to the window?"

"I'm not bringing it to you!"

He held up his hands. "No problem. I'll get it from the window. Let's see. I'll need some strong string and a balloon."

I stared out the window. I had a feeling he was coming up with another one of his inventions to get out of doing work.

"You gonna help me, Squirt?"

"Do what?"

"Well, the little machine I've got in mind is based on one of Newton's laws of motion, so I guess I'll call it a Newtonizer."

I started to close the window, but I just couldn't ignore Eric's Newtonizer. I have a lot of what Mom calls scientific curiosity.

"OK," I called. "String and a balloon."

"And a straw and masking tape," he yelled back.

I glared at him, but I got them anyway. Now that my scientific curiosity was stirred up, I had to know what a Newtonizer was.

When I took everything out to the hammock, Eric was lying back reading his magazine. He looked up at me. "First, you have to thread the string through the straw."

By the time I'd finished, Eric had another instruction for me, then another. I stood on tiptoe and tied one end of the string to a nail on the windowsill and the other end to the big tree by the hammock. The string looked like a skinny clothesline, except it had a straw on it.

Eric cut a short piece of string and tied a big paper clip to one end. I taped the string to the straw, letting the paper clip hang down a few inches.

But the part that really baffled me was the balloon. I blew it up as big as I could. Then, while Eric pinched the end shut, I taped the balloon to the straw.

Talk about weird looking! But I knew from experience that the Mad Scientist wouldn't answer any questions, so I didn't bother asking.

"OK," Eric announced. "The Newtonizer is now ready. Bring my soda to the kitchen window."

I ran inside, stopping by the door to look at my mad-scientist brother. He was still holding the end of the balloon and moving the straw back and forth on the string.

Grabbing a soda from the refrigerator, I went over and leaned out the window.

"Ready!" I hollered.

Eric let go of the balloon, and the air whooshed out. The straw started moving, faster and faster, racing up the string toward the window. I stared as the balloon shriveled into nothing and the straw slid to a halt inches from the window.

"Hook it on!" Eric yelled.

"Hook *what?*" I asked.

"The can. Hook the paper clip through the hole in the can's flip top."

I pulled the end of the paper clip through the hole in the flip tab. When I let go of the can, it hung down from the string like a little cable car.

Suddenly, it moved. The straw and the can of soda hanging down from it were sliding down toward Eric as he waited by the tree. A second later I heard a pop as he opened the can.

The Newtonizer had done its work—or, rather, Eric's work. I laughed, then ran outside.

Eric looked up at me from the hammock. "Newton's third law of motion," he explained. "For every action—the air rushing backward out of the balloon—there's an opposite reaction—the straw pushing forward along the string. Then simple gravity brought the can of soda to me."

"That's pretty good," I admitted, "except for one thing. All this"—I waved my hand at the shriveled balloon hanging from the straw—"took you more energy than just walking into the house and grabbing a soda."

"No, it didn't."

"Sure, it did. You had to get the balloon and the straw, the paper clip, the string . . ."

"*I* didn't get them. *You* did, Squirt."

"What?"

He grinned. "It wasn't my energy that built the Newtonizer. It was yours."

My mouth fell open. He was right! I'd built the whole thing and done all the work for him.

Eric started laughing, which was a big mistake. I grabbed the edge of the hammock and pulled up hard. The hammock flipped over and dumped Eric on the grass. Luckily for him, the grass was thick and soft, since he still hadn't mowed it.

"Simple gravity," I announced smugly.

"What *about* gravity?" he demanded.

I laughed. Eric wasn't the only one who could use the laws of nature to do his work for him.

"Gravity," I told him, "is what landed you in the grass and saved me the trouble of working to get even!" He groaned, but I just smiled. A family could have more than one mad scientist.

To the Moon on a Sea Horse

By Trinka Enell

Erin tucked a blanket around her little brother, Joshua. "I'll tell you a story," she told him, "if you promise to go to sleep without fussing."

"A moon story?" he asked. "I like moon stories!"

Erin thought for a minute. "Sure," she said. She leaned against the wall and began. "Once upon a time, when I was as small as you are, I flew to the moon on a sea horse."

"A sea horse?" said Joshua. "Why didn't you go in a spaceship?"

"Joshua, I like sea horses!" Erin said. "Do you want to hear this story or not?"

"I'm sorry," Joshua said. "I won't interrupt."

"Good!" said Erin. "Anyway, I flew to the moon on my beautiful pink-and-purple-striped sea horse to look for precious jewels."

Joshua sat up. "All right! Did you find some?"

"Yes, I did," Erin said. "I found hundreds of rubies in a deep, dark hole. So I got off my sea horse and slid into the hole—"

"But, Erin," said Joshua, "why didn't you fly the sea horse into the hole?"

Erin glared at her brother. "He's scared of dark holes," she said. "Will you please hush?"

"OK," Joshua said in a small voice.

Erin sighed. "Anyway," she said, "I slid down the hole and scooped up hundreds of rubies. I stuffed them into my pockets."

"It's a good thing your space suit had pockets," said Joshua.

"I wasn't wearing a space suit!" Erin gritted her teeth. "I was wearing a white lace jump suit with fifteen pockets. And after I filled them all up, I tried to climb out of the hole. But I was too heavy, and I kept slipping back. Finally, I asked my sea horse to hang his tail down into the hole. Unfortunately, I couldn't reach it."

"Oh no!" Joshua cried. "Did you have to stay in that creepy dark hole for years and years?"

Erin shook her head. "No, Joshua, I didn't. I couldn't reach his tail—"

"You said that already," Joshua interrupted.

"Joshua!" Erin said. "Hush up or I'm leaving! Then you'll *never* hear the rest of the story."

Joshua pulled the blanket over his head. "Sorry," he mumbled.

"I hope so," said Erin. "Now where was I? Oh, I remember. Since I couldn't reach my sea horse's tail, I pushed the rest of the rubies into a big pile. Then I struggled up the pile, grabbed his tail, and tried to pull myself up. But instead I pulled my sea horse into the hole."

"Wow!" said Joshua. "What did you do then? Did you make a bigger pile, climb up, and drag your sea horse up behind you?"

"No, I didn't, Joshua!" Erin cried. "I yanked the rubies out of my pockets and dumped them on the ground. Then I was light enough to jump on my sea horse, and we flew out of the hole."

Joshua groaned. "You mean you left all the rubies in that deep, dark hole?"

"Yes!" Erin said. "Otherwise I would still be stuck there. Would you like that?"

"No, Erin," Joshua said. "But did you have to leave *all* the rubies?"

"Well . . . ," said Erin, "not every single one. I thought I should eat before we left the moon, so I got a cream-cheese-and-banana sandwich out of my pocket. I took a big bite. My teeth crunched into something hard. It was a gigantic ruby."

Joshua leaped out of bed. "All right!" he shouted. "Where is it?"

"Joshua," Erin said, "you'll never know unless you get back into bed and stay there."

She waited until he was settled, then went on with the story. "I wiped off the ruby, put it in my top pocket, and finished my sandwich. Then we flew home. It was a splendid trip."

"But what about the ruby?" Joshua asked.

Erin just looked at him. "When I got home," she said quietly, "I emptied my pockets looking for the ruby. But all I found was a big red rock."

"What!" Joshua screeched. "You lost the ruby? Oh, Erin!"

Erin leaned over and whispered to her brother. "You're supposed to be getting sleepy," she said. "And you're not supposed to be yelling."

Joshua frowned. "All right. I'm sorry. I won't yell anymore, but please finish the story."

"OK," Erin said. "No, I didn't lose the ruby." She pulled a rock from her pocket. "This is the ruby. You see, moon rubies are rubies only when they're on the moon. On earth, they're just plain old red rocks."

Joshua moaned. "You mean you went through all that just for a rock?"

"Yes, I went through all that just for a rock," Erin said. "Now will you please go to sleep?"

"OK," Joshua said. "Thanks for the story." He curled up and closed his eyes. "I'm sorry all you got was a rock, Erin," he whispered.

Erin smiled and shook her head. "Oh, Joshua," she said softly. "Someday you'll go to the moon. Then you'll come back and tell *me* stories."

But Joshua was already asleep. Erin pulled up his blanket, kissed him good-night, and turned off the light.

I Caught a Salamander!

By Christine Harder Tangvald

"I caught a salamander!" Natasha shouted as she rushed through the door. "Mom, come outside and see Fred."

"You caught a *what?*" Mother asked.

"A salamander," Natasha said.

She showed her new pet to her mother. Fred, the salamander, was looking out of a peanut-butter jar half-filled with sand, mud, and weeds.

"Isn't he wonderful? I found him crawling in the grass down by Rock Creek. He seemed to be lost, so I brought him home."

"He does look like a nice salamander," Mother said, "but what are you going to do with Fred now? You can't leave him in a peanut-butter jar forever. And what are you going to feed him?"

"I think salamanders like flies and worms," Natasha said.

Mother pretended to look sick. "Who is going to catch these flies and worms?"

Just then Justin, Natasha's brother, came crashing through the door, carrying a baseball and mitt.

"Whatcha got there?" he asked as he dropped his mitt and ball onto a chair.

"My new pet salamander," Natasha replied. "I found him down by Rock Creek, and I've named him Fred."

"Cool," Justin said as he let his jacket and hat fall on the floor. "Let me see him."

Justin and Fred looked at each other—one from outside the peanut-butter jar and one from inside. Fred's dark skin was smooth and moist. He was about four inches long, had four legs, and looked sort of like a lizard. His tail was long and pointed.

"He's neat," Justin said, "but let's fix him up in that big gallon jar I found in the basement. We can put some rocks and stuff in it for him."

"Great," Natasha said.

"We learned about salamanders in school," Justin went on. "Some live in water, and some on land. Lots of people think salamanders are lizards, but they aren't. In fact, salamanders will shrivel up and die if their skin dries out, so we have to keep Fred good and damp."

Off they went to get the big jar. They put mud and sand and plants in it. They put holes in the lid. They caught two flies and dug up some worms for Fred to eat.

When they had taken care of Fred's new home and cleaned up the mess, they washed their hands. Natasha told Mother, "I didn't know it would be so much work to take care of Fred."

Mother replied, "When you have a pet, it's your job to provide a good home for it. I'm glad you and Justin are willing to take good care of Fred. May I ask you one favor, though? Please don't take off the lid and let Fred crawl around in *my* kitchen."

They all laughed. Mother gave Natasha a big hug. Then she gave Justin a big hug. She did not, however, give Fred a big hug!

The next day Natasha noticed that Fred had not eaten the flies or worms.

Maybe he isn't hungry yet, she thought. All through the day she watched Fred. He didn't eat. He just ran back and forth in the big jar.

Justin and Natasha caught more flies for Fred. He wouldn't eat them either.

The next day Fred did not run back and forth in his jar. Fred sat very still.

"What's the matter, Mother?" Natasha asked.

"Most animals prefer to catch their own food," Mother said. "Many times animals that are taken away from their natural home will not eat."

Natasha looked at Fred. "I don't think he likes it here. Do you think he'll die? I don't want him to die. What should we do?"

"I've seen lots of salamanders around Manito Pond," Justin said. "Why don't we turn him loose and let him catch his own food?"

Natasha thought quietly for a minute.

"I like having a pet," she said, "but I don't want him to die. If he would rather be near a pond, then that's where we'll put him."

Mother drove Justin and Natasha and Fred down to Manito Pond. Natasha took Fred out of the jar and gently set him on a small rock. Fred sat there. He didn't know he was free.

Justin gently touched Fred's tail with a stick. Suddenly, Fred scurried off the rock onto the ground. His legs and tail and body wiggled as he ran through the grass toward the pond. As he disappeared behind a big stone, his tail gave one last wiggle as though to say, "Thanks for setting me free!"

"He loves it here," Natasha exclaimed. "I'm glad we turned him loose."

Natasha was happy. Justin and Mother were happy. But most of all, Fred, the salamander, seemed to be happy.

My Foster Sister

By Heather Klassen

I am standing on the front porch, not wanting to go inside. I know the foster child is in there. I guess I should call her by her name.

Lisa. She's twelve, same as me, and her family is going through some hard times. Mom and Dad told me about her two weeks ago, when they told me they had decided to take in a foster child.

"Sarah, is that you?" My mom's voice floats through the screen door. She's heading my way. But I'm not ready to go in. I dart behind the hedge bordering the porch. My mom pokes her head out the door, doesn't see me, and calls to someone inside. "I guess that wasn't Sarah after all. She should be here any minute."

I plop down beside the bush. I'll have to go inside eventually, but I can't help putting it off. The whole thing doesn't seem fair. When they told me about their foster child idea, Mom and Dad wanted to know how I felt about it. What could I say? Even though I knew it was a nice thing to do, I didn't like the idea of sharing my home—not to mention my parents—with a stranger. But I don't like to disappoint my parents. So I said it sounded fine, even though it didn't.

Might as well get it over with. I stand up, fling my backpack over my shoulder, and tramp up the steps. Mom meets me at the door.

"There you are, Sarah," Mom holds open the screen door. I step in and glance around the living room. It's empty.

"Lisa's in the kitchen. She'll be out in a minute." Mom puts her hand on my shoulder and leans toward me. "I think she's feeling a little nervous. I'm counting on you to help her feel comfortable, Sarah," she says quietly.

I hear ice cubes clinking into a glass while I wait for Lisa. The questions I've been asking myself for the past two weeks keep circling around in my head. What if she picks fights with me? Or steals my stuff? She's from another part of the city, where no one I know lives. The problems in her family are so bad that she has to live here for a while. Her life sounds so different from mine. What could we possibly have to talk about?

Just as I'm about to ask my mom something, Lisa walks through the doorway into the living room. She stops when she sees me. Lisa looks just like I knew she would. She is different from me and my friends.

Her blond hair is cut short, and she must have three earrings in each ear. She's even wearing makeup. I wonder what my mom thinks of that!

And her clothes. None of my friends would ever wear an outfit like that. A baggy, ripped sweatshirt and paint-splattered jeans. Boys' black hightops without laces.

Mom nudges me in the back. I know I'm supposed to say something. "Hi, Lisa. I hope you like it here."

Lisa nods slightly and takes a sip from her glass.

"Sarah, I told Lisa that you'd show her to her room and help her unpack."

"Sure," I say. I pick up Lisa's suitcase and carry it to the stairs. Lisa sets her glass on an end table and follows me. We go upstairs and down the hall to the guest room. Now it's Lisa's room.

"I'll just put your suitcase on the bed," I say.

"OK," she mumbles.

I sit on the edge of the bed and watch Lisa as she opens her suitcase. She pulls out a stack of clothes and dumps them on the bed. I'm wondering if any of her clothes are all in one piece when I notice part of a book sticking out from a pile of clothes. The cover looks familiar. Not thinking, I reach over and pull out the book.

"Have you read that?"

Startled by Lisa's first complete sentence to me, I look up at her. "Are you kidding? This is my favorite book. I must have read it ten times!"

"Is that all?" Lisa sits down next to me. She takes the book from me and runs her fingers over the cover. "I just had to bring it with me. It is my favorite book, too," she says softly. "I'm really surprised you like it."

"What do you mean?"

"Oh, you know. The way you are." Lisa seems to fumble for the words. "Your parents, and your clothes and all." She turns back to her unpacking.

I scan my outfit. A pink sweater over a turtleneck, new jeans, and pink running shoes. Nothing wrong with my clothes. They're the same as my friends wear. They're different from what Lisa's used to, I guess.

Thinking about my clothes, I suddenly realize why Lisa hasn't smiled since I met her. I have to share my parents and my house, but she has to get used to everything being new and different.

Including me. It must be harder on her than it is on me. And she knows less about me than I do about her. But I do know that we both like the same book.

"Remember the part where the two girls get stuck in the cave?" I blurt out.

Lisa laughs. "And the part where the guy goes running down the hallway after them?"

We both laugh.

"Have you read any of her other books?" I ask.

"I didn't know she wrote any more."

"Oh, sure, lots. I have the whole series. Do you want to borrow them?" I ask her.

"If it's OK with you."

"It is." I jump up from the bed and head for my room. As I'm pulling books from the shelves and thinking how much we'll enjoy talking about them, something really nice occurs to me. Mom and Dad are getting a foster child, but maybe—just maybe—I'm getting a friend.

Katy and the Kite

By Nancy Garber

Katy picked up the kite carefully, now that she finally had it back together. Oh, she'd had it bowed and strung before. But then Matt, her little brother, came along on his roller skates. He rolled right over it and tore it in three places.

Of course, he hadn't meant to. And when she'd yelled at him, he'd even cried. That made her feel bad, but after all—why wasn't he more careful?

"He's only five, you know," her mother said. "And accidents do happen."

So Katy had glued and pasted and taped and strung and used everything but bandages to put her kite back together. Now it was ready to go—she hoped. She tied the ball of string to the front of it.

"Katy," Matt called, "If I came along, I could—"

"Oh no, thank you," Katy said. "I can fly my kite by myself."

She went out the door. She licked her finger and held it up to the wind. There wasn't much cooling—meaning the wind was not blowing very hard. But enough, she hoped, to get the kite up into the air.

She held the ball of string in her left hand and the kite in her right. She ran into the wind, let the kite go, and watched it. It bounced, it bobbled, it swooped, it dived, and all the time it never went more than ten feet in the air.

Katy stopped. I must not be doing something right, she thought, but what? She leaned over and put her hands on her knees, panting for breath. She had run two blocks, and still the kite wouldn't go up. If she ran any farther in this direction, she'd be practically downtown. Katy stuck up her wet finger again, and, yes, the wind was still coming from the north, so it wouldn't do her any good to try to fly the kite on the way home.

She walked back, winding string and adjusting the front bowstring on her way. And when she got there, she saw Matt sitting on the porch steps, chin in his hands, watching her.

"Couldn't get it to go up?" he asked her.

"No," She said.

"Too bad," he said.

"Don't get smart," she said.

"I wasn't. Really. I was just saying that it's too bad. If you'd let me, I could—"

"Now, Matt. You already ruined it once."

She held the kite as she had the first time and ran, looking back over her shoulder. She could feel the wind, tugging, pulling, trying to take the kite from her. At last it was ready to fly.

She let the kite go with a push, up into the air.

And she fell over the stone wall into Mrs. Van Horn's vegetable garden, landing right in there with the carrots and the lettuce.

The kite crashed down on top of her, and the ball of string rolled out of her hand and under a tomato plant.

Katy stood up, brushed off her jeans, gathered her kite and string (and a cucumber by mistake). She apologized to Mrs. Van Horn, who was standing right there, looking at her crunched vegetables.

"That's all right, dear," she said.

Katy knew she was just trying to be nice. "I feel awful about it," she said. "If I can do anything—" She handed back the cucumber.

"No, dear, really, it's all right," said Mrs. Van Horn. "You couldn't help it. Accidents do happen."

"Yes," Katy said. "They do." And she thought about this on the way home.

When she got there, Matt was still sitting on the steps, chin in his hands, skates on his feet.

"Hey," she said. "I need you."

He jumped up. "You do? Me?"

"Sure," she said. "Here, you hold this string. No, wait. I'll hold the string and you roller-skate as fast as you can, with the kite, down the block that way. Then when I yell, you let go and give it a push into the air. OK? See, I'll be running along with the string at the same time."

So Matt skated down the block. When Katy hollered, he threw the kite into the air as high as he could, and Katy could feel the pull on the string. "Go up," she called to the kite. "Go on up!"

And the kite went as high as the tops of the lilacs, then on up to the tops of the trees, then—swooping and pulling—up even higher, almost to the clouds, climbing, climbing.

"Yay!" Matt called, sliding to a stop beside her. "You did it!"

"We did it, you mean," Katy said. "I couldn't do it alone."

"Really?" he said.

"I mean it. You helped. And I'll tell you something else, Matt. I'm not mad at you anymore because you tore it before."

"You're not?"

"No. Accidents happen, you know. Here, want to hold the string?"

"You mean it?"

"Sure." She took the end of the string and started to wrap it around his wrist so that, even if he let go, the kite couldn't get away. And as she was just about to tie a knot, Katy sneezed.

And she dropped the ball.

And the last of the string came loose from Matt's wrist and flew up into the air.

As they stood there, Katy and Matt watched the kite get smaller and smaller and smaller as it went farther and farther up and away.

"Well," Matt said, "accidents do happen." And they started to laugh.

Goofy Patricia

By Paul D. Pitts

"You're goofy, Patty," I said. As usual, my older sister just looked at me, shaking her head.

"You're still such a child, Jeffrey." She knows I hate to be called Jeffrey. My name's Jeff.

Patty hasn't always been goofy. It started when she changed her name to Patricia.

"I'm too old for 'Patty' now," she said. "When you're thirteen, you'll understand, Jeffrey."

"Jeff," I said. "Call me Jeff."

Today, I was sure she was goofy. The box in my hand said, "Salon de Marie Hair Color, Number 214, Elegant Ebony."

"Mom's going to kill you," I said.

"Oh, Jeffrey!" She looked at herself in the mirror. "Brown hair is for infants. Black will look so much more mature."

The lady on the box looked mature all right, but how would my sister look?

"Mom's going to kill you," I said again.

"She won't when she sees how beautiful I look and realizes that I'm not a *child* anymore."

"I'm sure she's not going to notice you spending three hours in the bathroom."

"We'll do it after school tomorrow while Mom is still at work."

"We? I hope you don't mean you and Marilou Stenson." She's just like Patty—busy being mature.

"No, Jeffrey," Patty said. "*We* means you and me. I don't want Marilou to see me until I've made the change from child . . . to woman." She piled her hair on top of her head as she spoke.

"Oh no," I said, standing up. "I am not getting mixed up in this thing. You change to a woman all by yourself." And I dashed for the door.

"Such a child," I heard my sister saying as I went to my room.

The next day after Mom left I heard Patty lock herself in the bathroom. While I worked on my model aircraft carrier, I wondered what magic was going on behind that door. Suddenly I heard a loud shriek.

"Jeff?" Patty yelled. "Jeff, you've got to help me!"

"Just a minute, Patty. I can't leave this model right now."

"Hurry, Jeff. Please!"

Because she said "please" and remembered my name was Jeff, I left the model.

There stood Patty at the bathroom sink. Black dye oozed down her neck and across her face, dripping off her chin. Her hands were tangled in her hair, and little black rivers ran down her arms, splashing onto the counter.

When she saw me, she wailed, "Jeff, what should I do?"

"You're getting that stuff all over the place. Come on. Lean over the tub and I'll rinse you off."

For once she didn't argue. She just leaned over, and I turned on the water full force. After a few minutes, the water turned gray, then clear.

"Is the black coming off?" Patty asked tearfully.

"I don't think so," I said, handing her a towel. "Dry yourself and we'll have a look."

She rubbed her towel-covered head with Elegant Ebony hands. Then, turning to the mirror, she slowly lifted the towel. Her hair looked terrible, sticking up all over, but her face was worse. It was covered with gray splotches, and her eyes looked like spooky eyes in vampire movies. She started crying again.

"Come on, Patty," I said. "Maybe it won't look so bad after you comb your hair."

In a minute I said, "See, that's better."

She stopped crying. "Do you really think so?"

"Sure," I said. "If you like raccoons."

"What are we going to do?" she cried. *We* again.

"Let's go down to the kitchen. That lady on TV says you can remove stains with stuff right in your own house. Maybe we'll stumble onto something that washes out Elegant Ebony."

The TV lady always uses vinegar. Patty pinched her nose and I poured and rubbed it in. But none of the black came off.

"Maybe an egg shampoo will do it." I really liked cracking the eggs on Patty's head and rubbing the stuff in her hair and on her face. But it didn't work either. She still had vampire eyes.

I can't remember everything we tried: mustard, salad dressing, grape jelly, even plain old margarine. I was just going to pour some ketchup, mixed with olive oil and club soda, on her head when I heard Mom's car come into the driveway.

Looking at all the junk in the sink and on the counter, I said, "You're on your own!" and disappeared as Mom opened the door.

All I really heard was a shriek from Mom and Patty tearfully explaining the problem. Mom was too busy to look for me, and I'm smart enough to stay away from dynamite. I just listened at my door.

I heard Mom tell Patty to wash her hair while she called the beauty shop. In a minute she yelled, "Tomorrow at two? This is an emergency!"

I guess the lady believed her because she and Patty left.

I spent the rest of the afternoon cleaning up the mess. It was the least I could do.

When they got home, Patty's face was pale, but at least she didn't have black raccoon eyes anymore, and her hair was almost normal.

I asked her what happened at the beauty shop, but she said, "I don't want to talk about it."

I guess Mom didn't want to talk about it either because she didn't mention it to Dad.

One good thing came out of Patty's trouble. She doesn't act so smart anymore. Yesterday, Marilou Stenson came over. I went into Patty's room, and they were both sitting there acting *mature.*

"Can I borrow some nail polish remover?" I asked. "I need to get some paint off my desk."

"Jeffrey and his models!" Patty smiled at Marilou. "He's still such a child."

"The paint is black," I said. "Elegant Ebony is the color—to be exact."

Patty's face turned red. "However, Marilou, Jeff's much more mature than other young men his age."

I gave her a very grown-up wink.

The Box in the Barn

By Barbara Eckfeld Conner

Jason heard his mom calling him. Instead of answering her, he slipped deeper into the tall weeds behind his house. He closed his eyes, thinking of what he had done.

He had gotten up that morning in a good mood. Raspberry pancakes were on the table when he walked into the kitchen rubbing his eyes.

"After breakfast, Jason, I want you to go into town with me," Mom said quietly. "It's your sister's birthday, and we need to shop for her gifts."

Jason was eager to go, even if the gifts weren't for him. Buying presents was always fun.

As they drove to town, Jason couldn't help but ask the question that had been on his mind since yesterday when Aunt Nancy came. "What's in the box that Dad took to the barn, Mom? Is it something Aunt Nancy bought for Megan's birthday?"

"It's a surprise, Jason, and I don't want you going near that barn today. Do you hear me?"

Jason sat staring at the road ahead. He knew that nothing would change her mind. Only now he was more curious than ever!

Back home, Megan ran out to meet Jason, her eyes wide and excited. "Jason, Jason, I'm six years old!" she cried, jumping up and down.

"I know, I know." Jason gave her a big hug.

Soon the house was buzzing with excitement. Megan sat on the stool watching while Mom and Aunt Nancy prepared the birthday dinner. Dad wouldn't be back for at least two hours. Jason wandered outside, trying to think of something to do, but his thoughts kept returning to the box in the barn.

He started walking toward the barn, not at all sure what he'd do when he got there. He was hoping for just a glimpse of the box. Instead he heard a strange noise coming from inside the barn. He wished he could just turn back to the house, but his legs carried him into the barn. Jason saw the box. It was sitting between two bales of hay. He could hear loud, wailing cries. Leaning over, Jason carefully lifted the lid. There was the cuddliest puppy he had ever seen!

"You must be pretty scared, huh, fellow?" Jason said quietly as he held the wiggly dog. "Megan's going to love you!" He secretly wished the puppy was for him. After all, Mom and Dad knew that he had been wanting his own puppy. Probably Aunt Nancy didn't know that, and anyway Megan would be happy.

Soon Jason was playing happily with the puppy, and he forgot that he wasn't supposed to be in the barn. Taffy, their big brown horse, stuck his head in the window as if to say, "What's going on?" Jason jumped, remembering that he wasn't supposed to be there. The puppy ran off as fast as it could out of the barn and into the field. Jason stumbled out of the barn, looking wildly for any trace of the puppy. "Come on, puppy! Oh, please come back here!" he called, his eyes welling up with tears.

Now here he was, two hours later, hiding in the weeds. He'd looked everywhere, but the puppy was gone. He had ruined his sister's birthday.

"Jason! It's time for dinner!" Mom called even louder now. Just when he was determined that he was going to stay forever in the tall weeds, he heard his sister's voice.

"Jason! It's time for my party, Jason!" Megan yelled excitedly.

Jason rubbed his swollen eyes, trying to look normal. He couldn't ruin everything for her. "I'm here, Megan," he called.

"Are you OK?" she asked with genuine concern.

"Sure. Let's hurry." Jason grabbed her hand as they ran back.

As soon as they reached the house, the party began. Jason tried to pretend that everything was fine. When it was time to open Megan's birthday gifts, he sat in the big easy chair, hoping no one would notice him. Finally, Megan opened the last present in the pile.

"I'll be right back," Dad said.

Jason knew Dad was going to the barn. Megan would probably never forgive him for losing her birthday puppy. Everyone, even Aunt Nancy, would be angry when they found out the puppy was gone.

"Jason! Come here!" Dad called from the front yard.

Jason slowly got out of the chair. It was hard for him to move, but Megan grabbed his hand and said, "Come on, Jason! Let's see what Dad wants."

Jason followed Megan out the door. Mom and Aunt Nancy followed close behind.

There was Dad standing with the box next to him in the grass. "Jason, I want you to open this box and see what's inside."

Jason looked up and saw that Dad was smiling. He turned and saw that Mom, Aunt Nancy, and Megan were smiling, too. What would he say to them when there was nothing in the box? But as Jason looked down, he jumped back in surprise. The puppy looked up at him with sleepy eyes.

"Wow!" said Jason, bewildered.

"The puppy's for you, son," his father said.

"I thought you'd like a gift, too, even if it isn't your birthday," said Aunt Nancy, laughing.

The puppy jumped up, ready to play. Jason and Megan spent the rest of the day with the puppy.

Later, when he was getting ready for bed, Jason turned to his father and said, "You know, Dad, I feel bad about something I did today."

Dad waited patiently as Jason explained what had happened. "And I still can't figure out how my puppy got back into his box!" he added.

"Well, son, on my way home I saw your puppy running along the side of the road. I figured he had gotten out of his box somehow. . . . You must have felt terrible during the party," Dad continued. "I get the feeling you've learned a lot today." He pulled back the covers on Jason's bed.

Jason looked down at his new puppy, who was sleeping soundly in a basket by the bed. "Dad, I think I'll call him Buddy."

Dad smiled and tucked the covers snugly around Jason.

A Room of Her Own

By Jeanette Knapp

"I wish I had a room of my own, Mom," Anne said. "Jennifer has a window seat with flouncy curtains and a gorgeous pink bedspread and . . . "

Then Anne stopped. She almost wished she had not gone to play at her friend's house. Pretending they were detectives was fun, but seeing Jennifer's room made her jealous. Why did Jennifer get to have that beautiful attic hideaway room all to herself while Anne had to share a dull bedroom with two little sisters?

"I wish all of you girls had rooms of your own," Anne's mother said. She put a bowl of apples and a small cutting board on the kitchen table and sat down across from Anne. "When we bought this house, we planned to turn the garage into bedrooms. We didn't know we'd have to waterproof the basement and replace the roof first. Next spring we'll build the bedrooms, I hope."

Disappointment choked Anne. Next spring sounded like never. "I need a room now. I hate sleeping with Brenda and Casey."

"That's not what you thought when they were visiting Grandma. Don't you remember how afraid you were to sleep by yourself?"

That was true, Anne thought. Sometimes she woke in the night and had trouble getting back to sleep. As she hid under the covers trying not to hear strange noises, it was nice to know her sisters were close by.

"But I want a place all my own," Anne insisted.

Her mother began peeling the apples. "I don't have a room of my own either. Your father and I have to share."

"That's different," Anne said. "You and Dad are never in your room. I don't have anywhere to be alone. Brenda and Casey are always doing gymnastics or playing with their stuffed animals in our room. I really want a room of my own where I can read and do homework in peace."

Anne watched the long, thin strips of apple skin curl to the table as her mother peeled round and round each apple. "Can I do that?" Anne asked.

"Here," her mother said, giving Anne the peeler. "You peel. I'll cut and core. 'Many hands make light work.'" Anne groaned. Her mother was always saying funny things like that.

"What are we making?" Anne asked. Peeling apples was harder than it looked. The peels kept breaking in the middle.

"Applesauce. Brenda chose a good menu for her Valentine party. Everyone should like macaroni and cheese, hot dogs, and applesauce."

"Why does she have to have a party?" Anne asked. Soon the house would be full of shrieking little kids, for Brenda had invited her eight-year-old friends as well as some of Casey's friends, who were only five.

Her mother smiled. "Because, while you like peace and quiet, your sister likes excitement. And I'm glad you're different because I like the variety."

Anne smiled back. Sometimes she worried that something was wrong with her because she wasn't always having friends over as Brenda did or calling someone to go bike riding or sledding. She was glad her mother didn't mind that she liked being alone some of the time.

Anne had just completed her first unbroken apple peel when Brenda came upstairs from the basement. "Wow, that's cool," Brenda said when she saw that the apple peel stretched out more than a yard. "Anne, can you help me decorate?"

"Sure," Anne said. She loved to decorate.

"I want to hang these streamers," Brenda said, "but I can't reach the ceiling."

"You sure have a lot of these," Anne said, taking some crepe paper rolls from her sister.

"I had to buy the whole bag. Just use the red and white ones."

Anne got a ladder and taped up strip after strip of crepe paper. They fluttered when anyone moved. The effect was beautiful, like a shimmering curtain of color.

"Get dressed, girls," their mother called. "Your guests will be here soon."

Anne stood still, staring at the streamers. Casey raced upstairs. Brenda dashed to the steps, ran halfway up, and then turned to call down, "Anne, you'll help with the games, won't you?"

Anne didn't answer. The streamers made the play area seem like a separate room.

"Anne, please?" Brenda said.

"All right," Anne said. Her idea would have to wait until tomorrow.

The next day was Sunday. Unless the weather was good enough for picnicking, Sundays were usually boring. Anne's parents worked on the house, Casey and Brenda played dress-up or games, and Anne yelled at them to be quiet. But this Sunday Anne and her sisters shut themselves in their room. On the door they taped a sign that said, "Secret Project! Do Not Come In!"

Finally Anne went to the basement to get her mother and father. "Come see our surprise."

"You know, Anne," her mother said, "I've been thinking. You're welcome to use our room whenever you need a quiet place to work."

"Thanks, Mom," Anne said. "That's a good idea. But come see our room."

Casey and Brenda were standing in front of their closed bedroom door. "Ready?" Anne asked.

"Ready!" Casey and Brenda shouted and pushed open the door. Pink, yellow, and blue streamers hung from the ceiling, filling the room with color. The shimmering crepe paper divided their room into three sections. The streamers around Anne's bed were studded with tissue flowers. Rows of stuffed animals peeked from behind the streamers around Casey's bed.

"Mine is the Flower Bower," Anne said.

"Mine's the Cuddly Corner," Casey added.

"And mine's the Gym," Brenda said. "I've got the most floor space, so I can practice all of my gymnastic routines."

Anne smiled. "Isn't it great, Mom? Now we all have rooms of our own!"

Everything for Scotty

By Joyce Hunt

"It's not fair, Mom. You always have to stay with Scotty!" Jeff pointed angrily to the large crib where his older brother lay.

When Scotty was born, the doctors had told his parents that his brain would not develop as well as other children's. He would never be able to run and play. Although Scotty was two years older than Jeff, he hadn't learned to talk much. The main thing Scotty ever did was lie in his bed and watch Jeff, occasionally calling out "Jevvy!" when he wanted his brother's attention.

"But you promised to go shopping with me," Jeff went on. "I don't know what to get."

"I would if I could," his mother said, trying to sound patient. "But Mrs. Marks just called, and she can't watch Scotty. You know he can't be left alone. He has to be with someone who knows him and knows how to handle him. You'd better get going. Martin's closes at six. Pick out something that will make Scotty happy for his birthday."

Jeff turned away so his mother wouldn't see the angry tears that filled his eyes. "It's not fair," he muttered as he reached into his pocket to make sure the three dollars he'd saved was there.

"I know." His mother's voice was weary. "Scotty's different, and you must try to understand." Then her face softened into a smile as it often did when she talked about Scotty. "Scotty's different, but he's also very special in our family. Someday you'll see that."

Jeff slammed the door of their apartment and started downstairs. Scotty's birthday, Scotty's baby sitter, Scotty's happiness! Everything for Scotty! Well, he was sorry. There was just no way that he would ever see how Scotty was special. No way!

Outside, the street was busy. How different it was from the country home his family used to have, Jeff thought. He loved the country, and when they had lived there, he'd built up a nature collection. In it were eggs, nests, butterflies, bugs, and a lot of things that reminded Jeff of the outdoors. But he might as well forget the collection now. Just because the best school for children like Scotty was in the city, his family had moved to be near it. Jeff gave a small stone a hard kick. Again, everything for Scotty!

A few houses away Patrick and Mike Duffy threw a Frisbee back and forth to each other. Watching them, Jeff felt his tears return. Why couldn't he have a brother who could play Frisbee, he wondered as he crossed the street and started through the park.

The park was Jeff's favorite place in the city. It reminded him of the country, and as he walked through he kept his eyes downcast, alert for anything he might find to add to his nature collection. Suddenly a flash of red caught his eye. Bending down, he picked up a feather. It was such a brilliant red it seemed to glow. Jeff guessed it had come from a cardinal. It would be a great addition to his collection. He wrapped it in a clean tissue he had in his pocket, then he hurried to Martin's.

Once there, he made his way quickly to the toy department. It was filled with all sorts of exciting things, games Scotty would never be able to play, books he would never read, and balls he would never get outside to throw.

Then Jeff spotted the Frisbees. There were dozens of them in wild, bright colors, and with the three dollars he had, Jeff had just enough money to buy one. Scotty couldn't use a Frisbee, but so what? He could let Jeff play with it.

Jeff paid three dollars to the clerk, who put a bright orange Frisbee, just like the one Patrick and Mike had been playing with, into a bag for him. Jeff started home.

But as he left the store, he began to wonder about what he had done. Deep down inside Jeff felt ashamed. But there was nothing he could do now. He turned and walked slowly through the park.

His father had bought a cake for Scotty, and everyone sang "Happy Birthday" while his father helped Scotty cut it.

Then it was time for the presents. Scotty was sitting up now, strapped into his wheelchair. His mother had gotten him a new pair of pajamas. She held them up to make sure they fit, while his dad showed his gift, a music box with zoo animals that went around as the song played.

Then it was Jeff's turn. Hesitantly he held out his present. Not the Frisbee, which was still in its bag under his bed, but a small gift, carefully wrapped.

"Open it for him," said his mother. Jeff tore away at the paper as his parents looked on curiously. Out fell the brilliant red cardinal feather. Jeff held it out for Scotty to see.

"Jevvy!" cried Scotty. He reached a clumsy hand toward it. Jeff took the soft feather and ran it along

Scotty's hand. Then he ran it along his face, under his nose, around his eyes. "Jevvy! Jevvy!" Scotty giggled in delight. Then Jeff threw the feather up into the air just over Scotty's head. He watched as it slowly swooped down, gently floating like a tiny cloud until it landed on Scotty's lap. Scotty's eyes filled with wonder. "Jevvy!" He was laughing out loud. "Jevvy!"

When Jeff turned to look at his parents, his father was grinning. His mother said, "Looks like your gift is the hit of the party. I've never seen Scotty so excited."

The happy smile he saw on his brother's face gave Jeff a warm feeling. He remembered Patrick and Mike. Would either of them get so excited over a feather? He knew they never would, and although he didn't completely understand, he had an idea that this was what made Scotty such a very special brother.

"I'll watch Scotty while you clean up," he said to his parents. He took the feather and held it high over his brother's head. And the feather floated down—more gracefully than a Frisbee.

The Lost Snake

By Muriel S. Lipp

Joanna opened the door slowly, looking carefully before she stepped into the nursery school. The lost snake—where was it? She had not slept well last night thinking about it.

This was her first paying job, feeding the animals in the nursery school where her little sister Kristin went. It was Joanna's job to see that the two rabbits, three hamsters, two guinea pigs, and Jake, the black snake, had enough food and water. She liked taking the animals out and cuddling them. They were gentle animals, used to being held. Ms. Glazer, the teacher, taught the children many things with animals.

Joanna wouldn't think of cuddling Jake, though. She was afraid to touch snakes. She knew Jake would not bite—Kristin loved him and was always telling how she let him wiggle up her arm. Joanna was afraid to admit it, but she thought snakes were . . . well . . . creepy, and she got the shivers just thinking of them. She never even liked to touch snake pictures in magazines.

Yesterday she had noticed Jake was gone when she first came in to feed the animals. Where was he? His big aquarium with the tree branch and rock and the light to keep him warm was empty. Joanna could see that someone had not put the top on straight. Jake must have slithered through the opening.

Joanna worried that the teacher would think it was her fault that the snake got out. She was afraid he might eat the smaller animals. But the hamsters' aquariums had tiny wire net tops, too small for him.

She walked carefully from one cage to another, giving the animals greens and seeds and pellets. The guinea pigs squealed loudly for her to come and pet them, to give them some food.

Where would a snake hide? Joanna hoped she would find him before she had to tell someone he was missing. But even if she did find him, how in the world would she ever be able to pick him up—all three feet of him—and put him back in his glass house?

She felt a strangeness in the room. It was too quiet. She felt as though someone were watching her. Could it be snake eyes following her movements? Joanna shivered. She looked up above her at the shelves lining one wall. Plenty of places to hide. Could he be watching her from between two boxes? In the shadows?

Suddenly Joanna knew what she would do. She would go back home and get Kristin. Kristin had begged to come along with her, but Joanna didn't want to admit even to Kristin that Jake was missing. But now, she thought, why not?

Back home, their older sister Lindsey was playing a game with Kristin.

"I need Kristin to help me over at the nursery school," said Joanna.

"Oh, boy!" yelled Kristin, who always wanted to help her sisters. She jumped up and down with happiness.

"Can you keep a secret—not tell anyone?" asked Joanna as the two walked back to the nursery school.

"Sure, I won't even tell my dolls."

"Good," said Joanna. "I need you to help me find Jake, the snake. He got out, and I can't find him anywhere."

Joanna unlocked the nursery school door and stepped into the room with Kristin behind her. Kristin skipped over to the hamster cage.

"Hi, Sleepy," she said to her favorite hamster. Then she began looking for the snake under cages and inside shelves. Joanna noticed that Kristin was not a bit afraid, while she, a good seven years older, was not putting her hands inside anything for fear of suddenly touching Jake.

"Aren't you afraid to touch Jake?" asked Joanna. "Don't you hate the slimy way snakes feel?"

"Jake's not slimy," said Kristin loudly. "He's cool and nice."

The two kept looking, Kristin's little hands reaching everywhere trying to feel Jake. Finally Kristin said, "I know where he is," and she dashed out to the kitchen. In a moment she came back with an armful of black snake, part of him hanging down on the floor.

"Oh, good, you found him!" shouted Joanna. "Where?"

"Under the sink," said Kristin. "That's where he was before when we lost him. Ms. Glazer says he hunts mouses there."

"You mean *mice*."

"Mices," said Kristin.

Joanna watched in admiration as her little sister talked to Jake. Kristin let him wrap his body around her legs.

"Here, let me help you put him back," said Joanna. She was afraid to touch Jake, but she knew it was her responsibility to take care of him. And if Kristin could touch him, well, so could she. Slowly Joanna touched the snake's skin, and to her surprise it was cool and not at all unpleasant. Together the two girls lifted Jake back into his aquarium, gave him food, and secured the top.

"Kristin, you really were a help to me," said Joanna as they walked home. "I couldn't have found Jake without you."

The Warming House

By Bethea verDorn

"Does Carrie have to come?" my brother asked.

"Of course. She wants to skate, too. Just don't let her get too cold." Mother zipped my boots.

Then we were out the door—my big brother and I. We carried our skates, blades covered with rubber guards. My brother had his hockey stick.

"Now listen," my brother told me. "I have a big game today, so don't bother me."

He walked ahead and pretended that I wasn't following him. I followed him anyway.

The warming house smelled of wet wool and burning wood. Our cold cheeks grew warm once we got inside.

"Hey, Ben! What took you so long?" my brother's friend asked him.

"I had to wait for my sister," he complained. He didn't think I heard him. But I did.

I sat on a bench to take off my boots. The warming-house keeper threw a few scraps of wood into the stove, then bolted the heavy iron door shut. Wet mittens sizzled on top of the stove.

"It's very hot," said a lady to her young son. "Don't touch."

"Don't lose your skate guards again," Ben scolded me on his way out the door. So I tucked them in my boots and started to lace my skates. Why were there so many holes?

"Do you need some help?" asked the lady with the little boy.

I nodded. "Can you make a double bow?"

"Your brother should have helped you with these," the lady said.

"I know, but he has a big game today and I'm not supposed to bother him."

"Careful going down the steps," she warned.

I held tight to the railing and took tiny baby steps out to the rink. The ice was smooth and clear—except for a spot on the far side. Naturally, I fell there.

Next time I was ready for it. But I was not ready for the girl who bumped into me.

"Watch where you're going!" she shouted.

I wanted to say, "Watch where *you're* going!" Only I didn't. Instead, I stared at her gliding away, spinning like a top, making a million rings on the ice. Someday, when I didn't have to wear snowpants anymore, I would skate like that.

"Don't you want to go in and warm up?" the lady with the little boy called to me.

"Oh no, I'm waiting for my brother. He should be done soon." From the next rink came the stick-cracking, ice-scraping sounds of his game.

I watched the lady carry her son to the warming house, wishing for just a minute that she was carrying me. Then I skated some more. The lights above the rink came on, buzzing in the early dark. It started to snow.

If I kept moving, maybe it wouldn't seem so cold. Then maybe I wouldn't notice that I couldn't feel my fingers or toes, that everyone had gone home, that I was all alone on the ice. Maybe . . .

Just then the hockey game was over. My brother crashed through the gate, a scowl on his face.

"Better luck next time!" someone yelled.

He had lost his game.

Back in the warming house my brother didn't see me. Nobody did. So I sat by my boots, shivering, trying to untie my skates with fingers so stiff they would hardly move. Why had I asked the lady to tie a double bow? Hunched over my snowpants, I tried not to let the ache in my toes make me cry.

"Say, Ben, what's wrong with your sister?" my brother's friend asked.

"Oh, boy. I forgot she was here." Finally he saw me. "What's the matter with you?" he said. He still had the scowl on his face.

"I-I can't get my skates off. My hands are too cold," I whispered, not looking up.

"Wow. Mom told you not to get too cold." He scowled even harder.

I looked straight at him. "No, Mama told *you* not to let me get too cold." And then I cried. I cried because I wanted my brother to help me. Because I wanted him to be my friend—not to forget about me. And because I was still so cold.

Slowly his scowl disappeared. He untied my skates and began rubbing my frozen feet while the keeper put more wood in the stove.

My feet began to thaw. "I'm sorry you lost your game," I said.

"That's OK. We'll win next time." My brother zipped my boots. "I'm sorry you got so cold."

"That's OK. I only fell twice," I told him.

"Wow, Carrie, that's good." He smiled. "That's really good. Now let's go home."

He took my hand. I was warm again. And we walked home together.

Two Plus Three Equals One

By Beth Thompson

"Julietta Maxwell."

"Here."

"Arnold Morgenstern."

"I'm here, Mr. Billings."

"Vicki Peterson."

"Here."

There was a pause as Mr. Billings studied Vicki's student information card and then flipped through the stack until he found Julietta's.

"Vicki, I see here that you and Julietta have the same address. I remember you from last year, in Mrs. McQuaid's class—but, Julietta, you're new to Silver Valley School. Are these addresses correct?" Mr. Billings was clearly puzzled.

Vicki felt her face getting red and hot as the class giggled and whispered. She noticed that Julietta was staring intently at her books. Vicki wished that she could slide under the desk and out of sight. Why did Mr. Billings have to ask about it in front of the whole class?

"I, uh, well. . . . my mother married Mr. Maxwell, Julietta's father, this summer, and they came to live in our house. So we have the same address now." Vicki's voice was so low that it was almost a whisper.

"Oh, I see," Mr. Billings said. "Sisters! Well, that's great. And, class, we're going to be making charts of our family trees this year, so, Vicki, you and Julietta will be able to work together on your family chart."

Family! No, thought Vicki grimly. Just Mom and me—that's a family. Why, she hadn't even begun to call Mr. Maxwell "Dad." He didn't seem to mind, but Vicki had noticed that Julietta and her brother, Tony, were already calling her mother "Mom." Vicki always felt a twinge of jealousy when they did that. After all, Mom wasn't *really* their mother, was she?

Mr. Billings finished calling the roll. Just then, Vicki saw a note being passed back to her. It was from her friend Amber, who'd been away at camp all summer. It said:

> Why didn't you tell me you have a new sister? Is she OK or awful? Do you have to share your room now? Meet me at recess.
>
> Amber

She's not my sister, thought Vicki angrily as she crumpled the note and threw it in the waste basket. And my room isn't really *mine* anymore.

It had taken so long to get her room just right, arranging horse figurines on the shelves and posters on the wall. Now some of the shelves held rocks because Julietta collected them and was going to be a scientist. Julietta's star maps hung beside Vicki's beloved horse posters. Nothing was the same.

"It's just that we're so different," Vicki told her friends Amber and Lisa at recess. "My mom keeps saying we'll be just like sisters, soon, but . . ."

"Yeah, it's pretty hard to have a sister just shoved into your life," Amber agreed.

"*And* a little brother!" Lisa added with a groan. "Well, things may be tough at home, but you've still got your friends. The three musketeers will never split up!" The girls linked arms.

"All for one, one for all!" Vicki shouted happily. Then she saw Julietta sitting alone on a bench, watching them. Vicki suddenly felt guilty that she was being so unfriendly. She was the only one Julietta knew at Silver Valley School. Julietta's friends were all back at her old school.

Vicki tried to push away the feeling. After all, her mom had chosen Mr. Maxwell, but she hadn't chosen his children. But Vicki couldn't keep herself from imagining how she would feel in Julietta's place. It was hard to ignore Julietta's loneliness.

"Vicki, Julietta, watch me!" a voice called across the playground.

"Who's that?" asked Amber.

"It's Tony, my, uh . . . Julietta's brother."

Tony was hanging by his knees from the climbing bars, grinning proudly, and Vicki had to smile. She watched Julietta walk over to Tony and saw them laugh together. They always seemed to enjoy each other, and sometimes at home she was the one who felt like the outsider. There had been just the two of them, she and Mom, for so long, and suddenly there were three more people in the house. Vicki wasn't sure who belonged anymore.

Julietta walked home with Tony after school. Vicki walked with her friends, chatting happily. But once inside the house Vicki felt awkward.

"Vicki, you and Julietta do your homework now," her mother said. "I have to grade papers for my history class tonight, so you two will have to team up to fix dinner." The girls nodded, not looking at each other.

Sitting at her desk, Vicki quickly wrote out answers to the questions in her language book. English was her favorite subject, and she always got A's. Then she stared at the page of math problems. She had listened in class, but math was so confusing. And she couldn't interrupt her mom to ask for help. But the first problem seemed impossible. She sighed.

Then she noticed that Julietta was staring miserably at her language book. The paper in front of her was blank. Suddenly Julietta looked up and said, "This homework is so *hard!*"

"It sure is!" agreed Vicki, and for the first time that day the girls smiled at each other. "Maybe I can give you a hand with the language assignment if you'd like," Vicki offered shyly.

Noticing the math workbook and the crossed-out numbers on Vicki's page, Julietta said eagerly, "And I could help you with math. That's something I *do* know—not like these prepositional phrases!" She laughed.

"Great!" Vicki said. "Then we'll have time to fix dinner. How are you at making tacos?"

"They're Tony's favorite! I'll grate the cheese," Julietta offered. And for the next hour, working together, the girls really felt like sisters.

When Mr. Maxwell came home, he called out, "What smells so good in here?"

"Tacos, Dad," Julietta answered. "Vicki and I made them together."

"And a chocolate pie," Vicki added. "Julietta showed me how . . . Dad."

Mr. Maxwell smiled broadly at Vicki. "Well, it looks like both my girls are good cooks. Shall I set the table?"

Vicki looked at the table, remembering how empty it had looked when there were only two places set. Actually, three more plates made it seem just right.

"Yes, please," Vicki said. "Set it for one . . . one whole family."

A Horse in the Kitchen?

By Peggy Althoff

Nick lowered his book. "Jill?" He waited until he was sure his ten-year-old sister was listening. "Come on outside with me," he whispered.

"Why? What do you want?"

"Just come on, and I'll tell you," Nick insisted.

"Why can't you tell me here?"

Nick, two years older than Jill, sighed impatiently.

Jill dropped her magazine on the table and stood up. "OK. OK. I'm coming."

They left their four brothers and sisters reading in the big kitchen.

Outside, Nick stopped and dug in his pocket. "Look," he said. Three cubes of sugar glistened in his hand. "I've got an idea." With a glance toward the kitchen door, he spoke softly into her ear.

Jill's eyes widened. "Are you serious? We're the oldest. We're supposed to be responsible!"

"Aw, come on," Nick scoffed. "You know it won't hurt anything."

"But Nick, why do you want to do a goofy thing like that?"

"I just want to, that's all. What's the matter, Jill? You scared or something?"

"No, I'm not, but what if we get caught?"

"We won't. You know how much Mom and Dad like to talk, and how they always help the other members with the dishes. They won't be home from church for a while, and we'll be done by then."

Jill hesitated. "OK, let's try it. But I'd like to know where you get these wild ideas."

Nick smiled and sprinted toward the horse corral. Jill ran after him, and together they scrambled over the gate.

Slowly, they approached the grazing animals. Sleek and high-spirited, the horses were originally wild from the Montana foothills. All but one.

Cob.

None of the children knew where he had come from. Shaggy, fat, and docile, he was a part of each child's earliest memories.

Now, as Nick came closer, Cob lumbered toward him. Nick pulled the sugar cubes from his pocket and held them to the horse's mouth. Cob eagerly nuzzled his hand, but Nick backed away. The horse followed.

"Go unlatch the gate, Jill. Don't open it till we get there."

After Cob passed through, Jill swiftly closed the gate. The other horses had already lifted their heads and started trotting toward the opening.

Cob, gentle and trusting though he was, hesitated when they reached the low, broad porch of the house. This was outside his territory, and he knew it.

"Give him a swat on the rump, Jill." Nick tugged on the horse's halter with one hand and reached for the kitchen door with the other.

Again Cob hesitated.

"Swat him again, Jill."

Another pat from Jill, another few steps, and there stood a horse in the kitchen.

"Ta-da!" Nick announced. "Behold the mighty mustang from the Montana mountains." He held the reins in his right hand, stretched out his left arm, and bowed from the waist.

The uproar from the children in the kitchen was exactly what Nick had hoped for.

"What are you doing? Are you out of your mind?"

"Wait till Mom and Dad find out."

"Get him out of here."

"What if he . . ."

Just then Jill let out a scream. "Mom and Dad! They're coming, they're coming!"

The children raced to the window. The car crested the hill less than a half mile away and loomed larger by the second.

Nick groaned. "We have to get Cob out of here. Come on, everybody!" He shouted orders. "More sugar, Jill. Len, get behind him. Hurry!"

Nick's brother flew from the window, yelling, "There's somebody with them." He jammed his shoulder against Cob's flank.

Nick pulled on the halter. "Come on, Cob. Come on—*move*!"

The others pushed.

Cob wouldn't budge.

The car stopped in front of the house. Four people got out.

"Oh no," howled Nick. "They're with Reverend and Mrs. Grant!"

The children froze like trapped rabbits as car doors slammed and steps sounded on the porch. The door opened.

"Hi, everyone," Mom began. "We . . ." With a loud gasp, she drew in her breath. Behind her, the wide-eyed Reverend and Mrs. Grant stood in shocked silence. Dad's usual welcoming smile changed abruptly to a stern frown. The children squirmed. Cob blinked.

"Whose idea was this?" Dad demanded.

Chins on chests, the children studied their shoes. The clock ticked, and Cob blinked.

"How could you *do* this?" Mom looked as if she was going to cry. "I've never been so embarrassed in my life."

"I'm waiting." Dad took a step forward.

All six children took a step backward. Reverend Grant coughed. Cob blinked.

"I'll ask you just one more time." Dad's voice was even and controlled. "I want to know—whose idea was this?"

They knew that tone of voice. This was serious. Nick raised his head. "Mine," he said.

"I helped," Jill added. The two children moved closer together.

Dad moved his level gaze from face to face. Gradually his stern expression softened. A sparkle came to his eyes. Then he threw back his head and laughed!

Mom smiled.

The Grants looked at each other. The reverend began to laugh, and soon everyone joined in. All except Nick.

"All right, enough of this," Dad said. "Go get a bucket of oats, Nick, and get this animal out of here."

"Yes, sir, right away." At the door Nick turned. "I'm sorry, Dad." He dashed out.

In the barn, Nick stood still, his face in his hands. His father's eyes—at first angry, then forgiving—burned in Nick's memory.

With tears of relief streaking his cheeks, Nick ran to the oat bin, scooped the golden grain into a bucket, and hurried back to his family—and the horse—in the kitchen.

A Gift of Feeling

By Barbara Schenck

Matt slowly counted the money in his hand. Two dollars and seven cents. No matter how many times he counted it, it was the same. And it was never enough. He stuffed the coins back in his pocket and sat leaning against the oak tree, staring at the sky. The book catalog under his arm dropped to the ground. He had wanted to buy his brother Steve a book for his birthday—a braille book because Steve was blind and was just learning to read braille.

"He's never had a book he could read himself," Matt had told his mother. "His very own book—to keep, I mean."

His mother nodded. "I know," she said. "You read to him so much, though, Matt. He likes that. And braille books are expensive. He's only going to be eight. There will be time for his own books later on." She laid a hand on Matt's shoulder and smiled at him.

Matt knew she was right. Steve did like it when Matt read him books and stories. But Matt also remembered something his mother did not. One night after he had finished reading to Steve, his brother remained still for a very long time. Then he said, "You love that story, don't you, Matt?"

Matt looked at the worn, often-turned pages. "Yes," he said.

"And it's there anytime you want to read it." Steve's voice was getting excited, and he sat up.

"Yes," Matt agreed.

"I wish I had a book," Steve said simply, and then he lay back down. "I wish I had a book that I could pick up and make the story come alive again, too. All these books are the same for me."

So it had to be a book—a braille book—because regular ones all felt alike to someone who couldn't see to read the words.

Suddenly, Matt sat upright. That's it, he thought. If a book didn't feel like the rest—even if it weren't a real braille book—wouldn't Steve be really able to know that book? His excitement grew, and the more he mulled over the idea the more he knew what he would do.

For the next few weeks Matt disappeared after school. He had a lot of work to do before Steve's birthday. During that exciting month he visited Steve's braille teacher, Mr. Gage; the librarian at the public library; and the hardware and art supply stores. Soon he had everything he needed.

Finally, the day of Steve's birthday arrived. That Sunday morning Matt was awake even before his brother. He got up quietly, dressed, and slipped outside to his dad's workshop. There he checked over Steve's present once again. Then carefully he wrapped the package. Tucking it under his arm, he went back into the house.

His mother was making waffles, Steve's favorite. "Good morning," she said with a smile. "Is that present for Steve?"

Matt nodded. He put it on the table by his brother's place with the other gifts.

"Where's Steve?" Matt asked.

"Right here," his dad answered as he opened the door to the kitchen. He and Steve were smiling as they came in.

"Happy birthday," Matt said. He caught his brother by the arm. "Do you want your eight swats now or later?"

Steve laughed. "Just try to get them." Then, sniffing, he said, "Mmm, waffles."

"Aren't you going to open your gifts?" Dad asked.

Steve went to his chair. He began opening his presents as Matt handed them to him. Matt saved his own gift for last. Mom and Dad gave Steve a jacket and a sack of red clay because he loved to make things with his hands. From his grandfather came the knapsack Steve had talked of but never dreamed of getting. At last Matt handed him a flat box. "This one's from me," he said. "Be careful. Don't just rip into it."

"OK," Steve said. Slowly he removed the wrapping. Mom and Dad looked at Matt questioningly. He smiled slightly at them but turned to watch his brother. Steve took the lid off the box and lifted out his gift. His hands moved quietly over it.

"A book," he breathed. His hands brushed the poster-board cover. "Hey!" he exclaimed. "Letters! I can feel letters. Is it sandpaper or what?" He stopped and slowly traced the letters on the cover—sandpaper letters spelling Steve. And after he had done it once, he did it again.

"It's *my* book," he said joyously, opening the first page. On heavy paper there were raised, cutout cardboard outlines of four people—a man, a woman, and two boys. *Steve's Story,* as Matt had written it carefully in newly learned braille, began at the bottom of the page.

Stumbling a bit, Steve read the two or three sentences on each page. He read that he always had eaten more graham crackers than Matt when he was little, and he felt the graham cracker Matt had glued in on that page. One page recalled their vacation at the beach and had sand, pebbles, and shells on it. Another told briefly of Uncle Bill's farm with glued-on corn, soybeans, and straw. On each page Matt had told the story in braille.

"I've got a book," Steve said as he closed the last page. "And it really is my own story. I can read it again and again, and I can keep it forever." He turned to where Matt was sitting at the table watching. "Oh, Matt, thank you. It's the very best gift ever."

Matt looked at Steve's smiling face, at his hands that still moved quietly over the cover, and knew it had been worth it. Steve's own book was worth every hour Matt had spent learning the braille alphabet, every error he had made transcribing the story with the stylus Mr. Gage had shown him how to use, every attempt to make Steve's story simple, yet alive and able to be felt and read by his brother alone.

"It was fun, Steve," Matt said. "I'm glad I made it. Maybe together we can make you a whole library of books!"

The Best Mistake

By Christine Miskovits

Kimberly Wilson was riding her bicycle when she saw a crowd of boys and girls in front of Stiller's Toyshop. Her younger sister, Lisa, was there, too.

"What's going on?" Kim asked.

"It's a contest," answered Lisa. She pointed to a jar that was filled with beans in the window. "Whoever guesses closest to the number of beans in that jar wins a toy worth fifty dollars."

"Gosh," Kim cried. "I wish I could win."

"So do I," said Lisa wistfully.

"You could never win," Kim said. "You're too little. Why you can't even count."

"I can, too," Lisa argued. "Today I learned how to count up to four. One, two, three, four. See?"

But Kim was paying no attention. She was staring hard at the jar in the window trying to judge its size.

"Come on, Lisa," she said suddenly. "It's time to go home."

"Aren't you going to try to guess at the beans?" Lisa asked.

"I've got a better idea," Kimberly said. "There are lots of jars in the cellar. I'll just find one the same size as that one, fill it with beans, and count them. Then I'll be sure to win."

"Can I help?" Lisa asked eagerly. "Remember, I can count to four."

"Well, maybe you can help me find a jar," Kim answered. "The sign says the contest closes tonight at six, so I don't have much time."

In the cellar, the girls searched for a long time without success.

"Why don't you just guess at the number of beans," Lisa said wearily. "I'm tired of looking."

Kim glanced at her watch. She didn't have much longer to get her entry to Mr. Stiller.

"Come on, Lisa," she said suddenly, dashing upstairs to the kitchen.

In the pantry, Kim found two boxes of dry beans just like the ones in the contest jar. "You said you could count up to four, right?" she asked while opening the boxes. "Put all these beans into piles of four. Then when I find the right jar, all I'll have to do is count the piles and multiply by four. Understand?"

Lisa didn't understand, but she did as her sister asked. "One, two, three, four. One, two, three, four." Little by little, Lisa filled the whole kitchen table with tiny piles of beans.

Some time later, when Kim came up from the cellar again, she was carrying a glass jar that looked the same as the one in Mr. Stiller's window. She carefully counted the piles that Lisa had made, multiplied by four, then put the beans into the jar until it was filled to the top. She had a handful left over.

After a little more figuring, Kim sat back with a sigh. "There," she said confidently. "That's it. The correct number of beans is 1140."

She pulled a sheet of paper from a pad in the kitchen and wrote her name on it. "Maybe I'd better print," she said thoughtfully. "It will be easier for Mr. Stiller to read. Give me the pad," she said to Lisa, who was busily writing on it.

Lisa handed her the pad, then picked up the sheet of paper with Kim's name on it. Once again, she wrote the only four numbers she knew—1 2 3 4.

Just then their mother came into the kitchen. "You'd better get busy with your homework, Kim. There's a Scout meeting tonight, and you'll be leaving right after supper."

Kim told her mother about the contest. "The store closes at six, and I have to get my entry in by then. The winner will be announced tomorrow."

Mother shook her head. "I'm sorry, Kim, but schoolwork comes first. You should have taken a guess at the number of beans instead of spending so much time looking for a jar and counting all of them."

Kim blinked hard to keep back the tears. "Can Lisa take my guess to the store?" she begged. "It's not dark yet."

"All right," Mother said. "But hurry, Lisa. Supper will be ready soon."

Lisa grabbed the paper and shoved it in her pocket. She ran all the way to Stiller's Toyshop and dropped it into the brown box near the window.

When she got back home, Kim looked angry. "You took the wrong paper," Kim shouted. She held up a slip of paper with 1140 written on it.

Lisa felt awful. In her rush, she had picked up the paper that she had been scribbling on. On that paper were written the only four numbers she knew—1 2 3 4.

Next day on her way to the playground, Lisa saw many boys and girls crowded around Stiller's

Toyshop. She knew they were waiting to hear who had won the contest. Lisa still felt terrible about her mistake. She wished there were some way she could make it up to her sister.

As she got closer to the store, Lisa could hear Mr. Stiller's booming voice. "There were several close guesses, boys and girls," he was saying, "but someone guessed the exact number of beans in the jar. Kim Wilson is the winner with her guess of 1234."

Lisa gasped. The paper she had put in the box by mistake had the winning number on it.

"But it's not fair," Kim argued when Lisa told her the news. "I didn't guess that number. How could I win?"

"But Mr. Stiller said your name," Lisa kept repeating. "He said you were the winner."

Mother interrupted with a suggestion. "Why don't you both go to Mr. Stiller and explain the mistake. That's the honest thing to do."

Kim and Lisa followed their mother's advice and went to Mr. Stiller. He looked very thoughtful for a few moments, then smiled broadly.

"Since it was Kim's name on the winning paper but Lisa who wrote the winning number, the best thing to do is divide the prize. You may each pick a toy worth twenty-five dollars."

Happy and satisfied, the girls walked up and down the aisles until they each had decided on a toy. When they were finally on their way home, Lisa hugged her shiny new skates and grinned. “I wish all my mistakes turned out this well,” she said with a laugh.